The Red Rock

A Graphic Fable

by
Tomio Nitto

GROUNDWOOD BOOKS   HOUSE OF ANANSI PRESS

The hill was steep. It always had been, but today Old Beaver felt very tired when he reached the top. He had come for his favorite view — the dams, lodges and ponds that filled the valley down below. He had built most of them during his long life.

"Good grief!" he said. "It's hard getting up here. Will I ever make it again?"

On the opposite cliff sat the weird red rock. It was huge.

It has always been there, always will be, thought Old Beaver. That rock felt like his oldest friend. "I'm not alone," he said to the breeze.

Bird song drifted up to him and he lay down for a quick rest. While he lay there dreaming, a meeting of developers was taking place in the big city, far, far away.

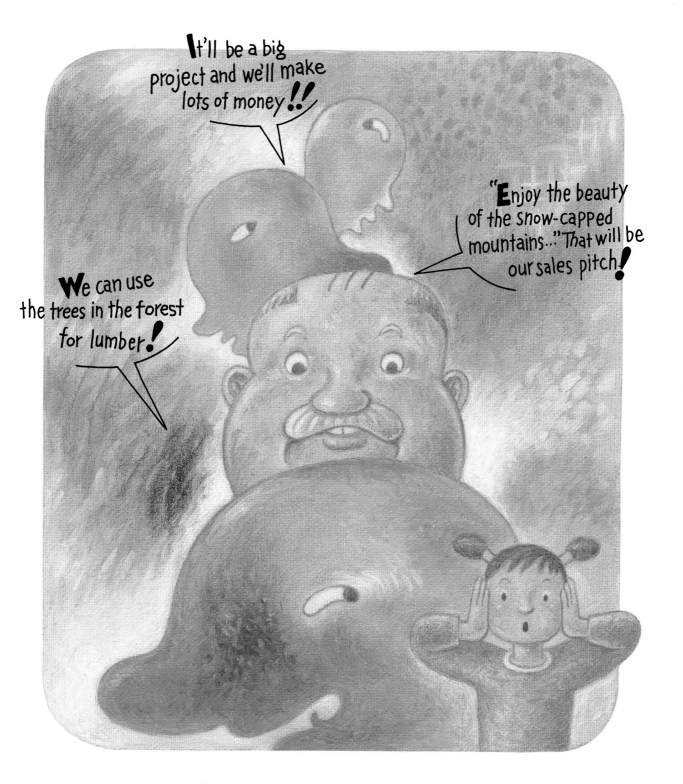

Voices shouted, "We've got to develop that empty space out there over the mountains. We'd be fools not to."

"Yeah, but that rock's got to come down. It gives me the creeps."

"I know," said the chief developer. "Let's put out a brochure."

That night a little girl saw news of this meeting on TV. What about the animals that live in that valley, she wondered. It's not empty.

WORLD'S BIGGEST SMARTEST PROJECT

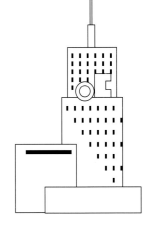

1   We'll construct a large dam where we'll float gorgeous cruise ships. We'll invite movie stars and rock stars and have special events, day and night.

2   We'll construct a luxury hotel on the hill and use plenty of electricity from the dam generator so it will be as bright as day, even at night. And we'll open a casino.

3   We'll bring down snow from the mountain and boil it to make a hot spring spa in the hotel. We'll call it "Long Life Hot Spring."

4   We'll carve the developer's face on the red rock and it will be worth a fortune. His great name will live on in history.

The Developer

snap snap SNAP

But the animals had no TV. They didn't worry when huge
boots began to tromp through the valley.

Only Old Beaver realized the danger. He felt a
little chill of fear.

It wasn't long before everyone was afraid. Trees were coming down so fast that even Old Beaver was astonished.

"I thought I was a good tree cutter," he mumbled. "But this is something else!"

Every day more homes were wrecked. Some animals died, and many others fled the valley. Those who remained sobbed, "What can we do?"

Old Beaver was fed up. He called a meeting.

"Those greedy guts just want our land to make money," snarled Wildcat.

"They'll never change," barked Fox. "They don't even know what nature is."

"Will they even notice when the nature's all gone?" growled Bear. "I doubt it."

"I just want to fight them," trembled Rabbit.

The little girl in the city had been thinking the same thoughts. She made a sign and held it up on the street corner. Then she planted some trees in her garden.

Old Beaver and Rabbit got busy organizing the
animals. The first step was to build barricades.

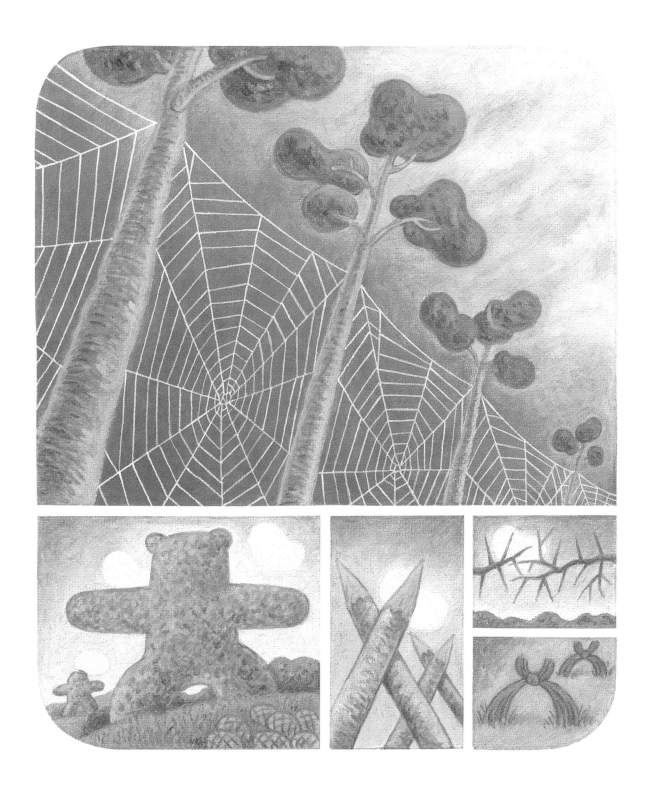

The spiders wove huge sticky webs. The squirrels built pine-cone warriors. The beavers built wooden fences with sharp tips. The deer draped trees with thorny ropes. And the very smallest animals built little grass traps.

But **ROAR RUMBLE CRASH!** The developers'
machines tore down their defenses in no time.

Owl hooted sadly, "We've *loooost.*"

"I'm afraid you're right," lisped Old Beaver. One of his teeth
had fallen out gnawing on a barricade.

The little girl felt terrible about
what was happening. Alone in her
room one night she looked out and
found the first star.

"Please find a way to save the
forest," she wished with all her might.

At midnight a bolt of light zapped out from the red rock. It seemed to know what to do.

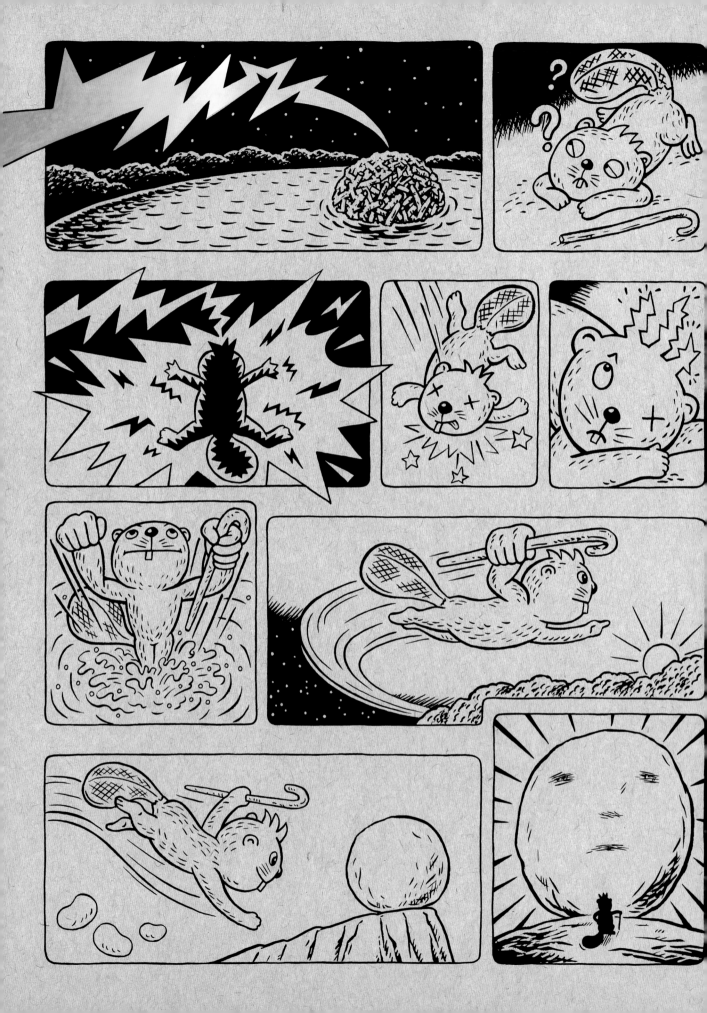

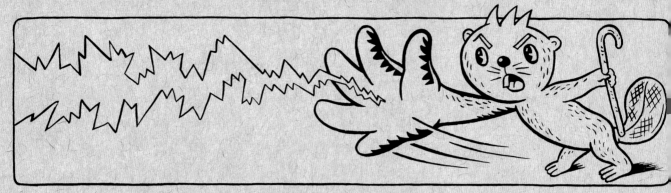
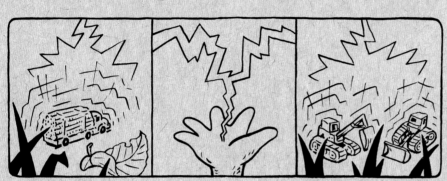

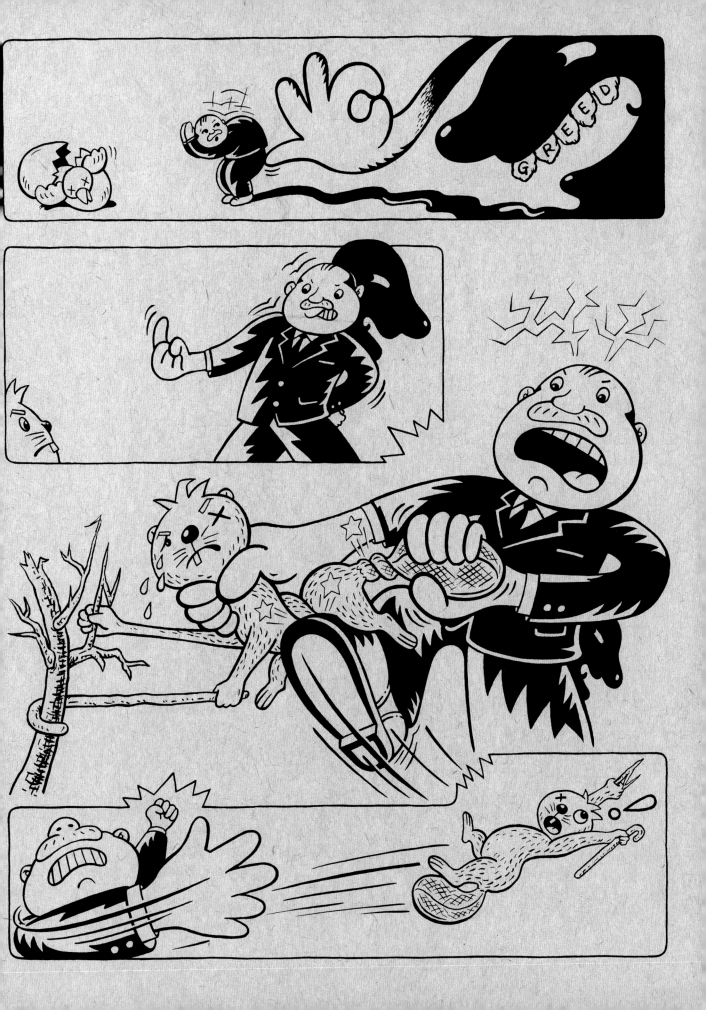

The little girl dreamed that the forest had grown back. When she woke up she found that her dream seemed to have come true.

"Wow!" "Yahoo!"

The animals were even more astonished to find that green trees were growing all around them once again.

"Yippie!"

Only Old Beaver didn't seem surprised. He just smiled gently, then told them what he had done. But he didn't tell them the whole story, which was that he wasn't really sure how the forest had been saved.

"You know, sometimes I think I just dreamed this whole thing from start to finish," he said to the red rock one day. The red rock didn't say a word, as usual.

For true or not, the animals learned what Old Beaver and the little girl and the red rock had always known — that you have to fight to defend this beautiful world. And you need friends by your side and all the help you can get.

And now you know it, too.

ACKNOWLEDGMENTS

Special thanks to Yuki S. Yamamoto, who helped me through the first stage of text translation. Also thanks to Joy Kogawa, Patsy Aldana, Michael Solomon, Bill Grigsby, Isabel Sousa, Gerry Mamone, William Wales, Gil Harrison and William S. Mizuno.

Most of all, I'd like to thank Canada. — T N

Groundwood Books / House of Anansi Press
110 Spadina Avenue, Suite 801, Toronto, Ontario M5V 2K4
Distributed in the USA by Publishers Group West
1700 Fourth Street, Berkeley, CA 94710

We acknowledge for their financial support of our publishing program the Canada Council for the Arts, the Government of Canada through the Book Publishing Industry Development Program (BPIDP) and the Ontario Arts Council.

ONTARIO ARTS COUNCIL
CONSEIL DES ARTS DE L'ONTARIO

Library and Archives Canada Cataloguing in Publication
Nitto, Tomio
The red rock: a graphic fable / by Tomio Nitto.
ISBN-13: 978-0-88899-669-5
ISBN-10: 0-88899-669-1
I. Title.
PN6733.N58R43 2005   jC813'.6   C2005-904838-7

The illustrations are in oil on canvas and brush and ink.
Printed and bound in China